STOL

Frank and Joe ran over to where Jason was standing. Seconds later, the rest of the team and Coach Quinn were there.

"What's wrong, Jason?"

Jason didn't answer Coach Quinn. He was red in the face. He kicked at the pile of gear.

"Tell us what happened, Jason," said Coach Quinn.

"My mitt!" said Jason finally. "Someone stole my lucky mitt. I can't play without it!"

The Jupiters heard the commotion and came over. Now both teams were there, surrounding Jason.

THE HARDY BOYS®

SECRET FILES #2

The Missing Mitt

BY FRANKLIN W. DIXON

ILLUSTRATED BY SCOTT BURROUGHS

ALADDIN ■ NEW YORK LONDON TORONTO SYDNEY

ALADDIN
An imprint of Simon & Schuster Children's Publishing Division
1230 Avenue of the Americas, New York, NY 10020
First Aladdin paperback edition April 2010
Text copyright © 2010 by Simon & Schuster, Inc.
Illustrations copyright © 2010 by Scott Burroughs
All rights reserved, including the right of reproduction in whole or in part in any form.
ALADDIN is a trademark of Simon & Schuster, Inc., and related logo is a registered trademark of Simon & Schuster, Inc.
THE HARDY BOYS is a registered trademark of Simon & Schuster, Inc.
For information about special discounts for bulk purchases, please contact
Simon & Schuster Special Sales at 1-866-506-1949 or business@simonandschuster.com.
The Simon & Schuster Speakers Bureau can bring authors to your live event.
For more information or to book an event contact the Simon & Schuster Speakers Bureau
at 1-866-248-3049 or visit our website at www.simonspeakers.com.
Designed by Lisa Vega
The text of this book was set in Garamond.
Manufactured in the United States of America / 0314 OFF
10 9 8
Library of Congress Control Number 2009932649
ISBN 978-1-4169-9394-0
ISBN 978-1-4169-9924-9 (eBook)

CONTENTS

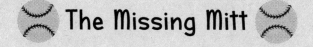

The Missing Mitt

1

The Big Game

The bases are loaded! Two outs, the bottom of the ninth. The Bayport Bandits really need this one to win." The announcer's voice was loud.

"Joe Hardy is stepping up to the plate, lucky bat in hand. His brother, Frank, is on third base, itching for home."

This was the most exciting World Series final anyone had ever seen. The crowd went wild. They were cheering and chanting, "Hardy! Hardy!

Hardy!" Eight-year-old Joe took a few practice swings. There had to be ten thousand people in the stands. Or more! He'd always dreamed of playing in the World Series. And now the Bayport Bandits had finally made it.

"If Joe can hit a home run, the Bandits will win this game. Otherwise, the Johnston Jupiters will be taking home the Commissioner's Trophy again."

The Johnston Jupiters were the Bandits' biggest rivals.

The crowd grew quiet as Joe got ready. He looked at his brother, crouched on third base. He gave Frank a thumbs-up. Frank was counting on him. The whole team was counting on him. Joe needed to hit this one out of the park.

The pitcher threw a curveball first. Joe let it fly by. It wasn't the right one. He'd never hit a home run off that one.

"Strike!" the umpire yelled. The crowd booed. Joe held up his hand. The crowd went silent.

The pitcher wound up again. This time the throw was high and inside. Joe swung, but he was too late and too low.

"Strike!" the umpire yelled again. This time, no one booed. The whole stadium was waiting.

Joe nodded at Frank. Frank got ready to run for home plate.

The pitcher threw the ball. It was perfect! Right down the middle of the plate. Joe took a big swing.

CRAAACK!

The sound of the bat hitting the ball was like thunder. Joe took off running. He didn't even look to see where the ball had gone. He knew he'd done it. It was the home run they needed. He had won the World Series!

The crowd was screaming his name.

"Joe! Joe! Joe!"

He rounded first base. His teammates were

jumping up and down. He looked over his shoulder. Frank had reached home plate. Joe made it to second base. Now the crowd was screaming even louder.

"Joe Hardy! You're going to be late!"

Joe shook his blond head of hair. The baseball diamond disappeared. He'd been daydreaming. He was sitting in the secret tree house that he and his older (by one year) brother, Frank, had helped their parents build. They were the only ones who knew about it—except for their mom and dad. He'd come up here to get his baseball gear and change into his uniform. Below, his mother was yelling his name.

"I'm coming!" called Joe. He picked up his backpack. Inside were his mitt, an extra uniform, and a snack. He climbed down the ladder to where Mrs. Hardy was waiting.

"I've been calling you for ten minutes," she said. She shook her head. "Go inside and eat some breakfast. The big game is today, you know."

As if he could forget! Today was the final game of the Little League season. The Bayport Bandits hadn't lost a game yet. But the Johnston Jupiters hadn't either. This was going to be the hardest game they'd ever played. Joe couldn't wait!

Frank was at the kitchen table eating Rice Puffs, his favorite cereal. Spread out before him was a large piece of paper filled with names and numbers. Joe grabbed a bowl and sat down next to him.

"What's that?" he asked. "Are you reading the phone book?"

"No," said Frank, swiping is dark hair away from his face. "It's the batting averages of the Johnston Jupiters. We've got to be ready for this game!"

Frank spent more time practicing with his brain than with his baseball bat. Joe was the opposite. Together, they were the perfect pair.

"They're pretty good," Frank said. "But none of them are as good as Jason Prime." Jason Prime was the star first baseman of the Bayport Bandits. He was the best player in the entire league. His father was Willy "Winner" Prime, one of the best pitchers in major league baseball. Jason was the reason the Bandits had made it this far undefeated. But Joe and Frank were pretty good too. Joe played second base, and Frank was the team's catcher.

Joe looked up at the clock. It was eight thirty. They still had plenty of time before the game began. They didn't even need to be at the park until nine o'clock. He poured himself a bowl of cereal.

"Good morning, boys," said Fenton Hardy as he walked into the kitchen.

"Morning, Dad!" said Frank and Joe.

Mr. Hardy took the clock down from the wall and unscrewed the back of it.

"What are you doing?" asked Frank.

"Mom says the clock stopped. I'm putting in a new battery."

Joe dropped his spoon. Frank stopped studying his paper. Their eyes grew wide.

"Oh no!" said Joe.

"It's almost nine o'clock!" Frank shouted, looking at his watch. Frank's watch could tell the time in ten different countries, and it had a compass, a calculator, and a tiny camera inside it. You never knew when those things might come in handy.

"Don't you guys need to be down at the park soon?" Mr. Hardy asked.

There was no answer.

"Boys?"

Fenton Hardy turned around just in time to see Frank and Joe rushing out the front door of the house.

2

Racing the Clock

Frank and Joe were in big trouble. Coach Quinn wouldn't let anyone on the team play if they were late for warm-up. Even their star player, Jason, had to sit out a game once.

"You have to respect your teammates," Coach Quinn had said. "And being on time is a way of showing respect."

Nothing would be worse than missing the biggest game of all. If they weren't at the park by nine o'clock, there'd be no championship for them!

They both put on their helmets. Joe's was blue and Frank's was green, just like their bikes. Then they hopped on and started pedaling as fast as they could.

"There's no way we'll make it!" said Frank. "It takes fifteen minutes to get to the park by bike. I know, I've timed it before."

"I know a shortcut!" yelled Joe. "Follow me."

Instead of turning left at the end of their street and biking down to Main Street, Joe turned right. Frank was right behind him. Soon Joe turned again, down a narrow alley between two big buildings.

"Whoa!" said Frank. There were garbage cans in the alley. It was hard to keep from knocking into things. A skinny cat ran between the wheels of his bike. He almost fell over twice.

The alleyway let out at the north end of Prospect Park. The baseball diamond was all the way on the other side. Normally the boys would have biked all the way around the park on the street, to get to the entrance at the south side. But today there was no time.

"This way!" called Joe.

The park was surrounded by thick bushes. Joe aimed his bike right at them. In a second he was going to run straight into them! Frank was about to yell for him to stop, when he saw Joe go right through the hedge. There was a small hidden gap. Frank followed Joe through the secret hole. He could feel the branches just brushing the sides of his face. That was close!

Now they were inside the park, at the top of the hill called Big Tree Hill. Below them were dozens of trees. Frank saw oaks and maples and pine. Then he saw Joe, flying between the trees!

Bump-bump-bump-bump!

Joe's bike rattled and jumped as he rode over

thick tree roots. He turned left and right. A few times he came within inches of crashing into the trees. But he never did. Frank was flying along behind him. He ducked to avoid a low-hanging branch. While he did, he checked his watch.

"We've only got seven minutes!" shouted Frank.

"We're almost there," Joe replied.

Finally they were out of the trees. Now they were in the big meadow, right by the baseball diamond. They were going to make it!

Suddenly something hit Frank in the back of the head! He lost control of his bike and fell into the field. Luckily, he was wearing his helmet, or he could have been seriously hurt.

"Ow!" he yelled.

Joe stopped his bike and ran over. A big stick was on the ground next to Frank.

"Oh no!" A voice came out of the woods. "I'm so sorry!"

An old man with white hair walked into the meadow. He walked slowly, with a cane. Beside him was a large yellow dog, which took one look at Frank and came running over. It looked like the dog was about to jump on Frank!

"Lucy! Stop! Down, girl!"

The dog ignored the man. She ran right past Frank and Joe and grabbed the stick in her mouth. Then she bounded away.

"We were playing fetch. You boys were riding so fast, I didn't even see you before I threw the stick. Are you okay?" The man sounded very upset.

Frank stood up, brushing the dirt off his pants.

"I'm all right," he said. He tapped on the helmet with his knuckles and smiled.

"Oh, good," said the man. "I'm Wilmer Mack. Everyone just calls me Mr. Mack. And you've already met Lucy. She's a good dog, just big and playful. She loves to play fetch. She'll chase after anything."

The boys introduced themselves and shook hands with Mr. Mack.

Lucy dropped the stick at Joe's feet. She wagged her tail, waiting. Joe took the stick and threw it as far as he could. Lucy ran off after it.

"Catch!" shouted Mr. Mack.

Catch? Suddenly Frank remembered why they had been going so fast in the first place. He looked at his watch—it was two minutes to nine!

"The game! We've got to go!"

He got back on his bike and started to pedal.

"Good-bye!" called Mr. Mack.

"Bye!" said the boys.

Ahead of them, they could hear the voices of their teammates at the baseball field. They were so close. They had to make it!

The boys burst out of the meadow and raced over to the bleachers. They could see Jason Prime and the other Bandits getting ready. But where was Coach Quinn? Were they already too late?

They jumped off their bikes and hurried to join their teammates.

"Hey, Joe. Hey, Frank!" Jason Prime gave them high fives.

Frank opened his mouth to ask if they were late.

TWEEEET! Coach Quinn's whistle blasted through the air. All the boys jumped to attention.

"Bayport Bandits, line up!"

They had made it in time!

3
Practice Makes Problems

A ll right, Bandits," said Coach Quinn. "This is going to be the hardest game we've ever played. The Jupiters haven't lost a game this season."

Coach Quinn was tall, with long red hair. She was the best coach the Bayport Bandits had ever had. She wanted them to win. But more than that, she wanted them to play well and have fun.

She called out their names and made sure every-

one was there. Then she divided them up into pairs to start practicing.

"Jason, you're with Joe. Frank, you're with Speedy. Now go warm up!"

Cissy "Speedy" Zermeño was the team's

pitcher. She was short, with dark hair and dark skin. She was known for her fastballs. In fact, everything about her was fast. She walked fast, she talked fast. She said it was because she was from New York City.

"All right!" yelled Speedy. "Let's do it, Frank. Come on! What do you think our chances are against the Jupiters? Have you seen them play before? I hear they're all really tall. They say Conor Hound is, like, six feet! And he's only in the fourth grade."

Speedy talked so fast there wasn't even a chance for Frank to answer her. But he didn't mind. He liked Speedy. Most of the time, even when he could get a word in, he didn't say anything because he was too shy. Frank was usually shy around girls. Joe was always the loud one.

Joe, Frank, Speedy, and Jason all went over to one end of the field. They practiced sliding into the bases, pitching, catching, running, and swing-ing. They did everything they could think of to get ready.

Right before throwing one of her special fast-balls, Speedy paused.

"Jason," she said, "Did you bring your lucky mitt? We can't play the Jupiters without it!"

Jason's lucky mitt was the one his father, Willy, had won during the final game of the last World Series he'd played in. It was Jason's good-luck charm. The whole team touched it before every game.

"It's in my bag," Jason said when Speedy finally stopped to breathe. "I'm saving it for the game."

"Phew!" said Speedy. "I was worried that— look!"

The boys all turned in the direction Speedy was pointing. A big silver school bus was driving up to the baseball field. Painted on one side was a giant planet. Frank knew it was Jupiter, the biggest planet in the solar system. It was also the namesake of the Bandits' biggest rivals, the Johnston Jupiters. The two undefeated teams would be playing each other for the first time all season.

The bus came to a stop near the bleachers. Out came the Jupiters, one by one. Speedy was right. They were big! Maybe not six feet tall, but big. And the biggest of all was Conor Hound, the Jupiters' first baseman.

Coach Quinn blew her whistle again. All the Bandits lined up to meet the Jupiters. They shook hands and promised to play fair.

The Bandits went back to practicing. The Jupiters put their extra gear in a pile on the other end of the field.

"Gosh, guys. They sure are big!" Speedy said. She looked even smaller compared to the Jupiters.

"You know what they say," said Jason. "The bigger they are, the harder they fall." Then he laughed. He didn't seem worried at all.

"Okay, get back to practicing! This game won't win itself!" Coach Quinn shouted. The team leaped to attention and went back to practicing.

Finally it was almost time for the game to start. Coach Quinn pulled out a large cooler from the back of her truck.

"What flavor do you think it is?" wondered Speedy. "I hope it's watermelon. That's my favorite!"

"It's orange," said Frank.

"How do you know?" asked Speedy. "It could be watermelon."

Frank shook his head.

"Frank's never wrong about these things," said Joe.

They waited in line. When, they got to the front, Coach Quinn handed them each a cup of orange-flavored water.

"How did you know?" asked Speedy, stamping her foot.

"Easy," said Frank. "I saw a stain from the orange powder on Coach Quinn's uniform. She must have spilled some on herself while mixing it."

Frank always paid attention to the small details. You never knew when they might tell you something important. His father had taught him that. Mr. Hardy was a detective, and he always told Frank and Joe to keep a sharp eye out. A clue could be anywhere. The brothers had already solved one mystery, and they were on the lookout for another.

All of a sudden, a shout came from the other side of the field. "AAAAH!"

Frank jumped, spilling the contents of his cup everywhere. He turned around.

Jason was standing by the pile of the Bandits' gear, screaming!

4

The Missing Mitt

Frank and Joe ran over to where Jason was standing. Seconds later, the rest of the team and Coach Quinn were there.

"What's wrong, Jason?"

Jason didn't answer Coach Quinn. He was red in the face. He kicked at the pile of gear.

"Tell us what happened, Jason," said Coach Quinn.

"My mitt!" said Jason finally. "Someone stole my lucky mitt. I can't play without it!"

The Jupiters heard the commotion and came over. Now both teams were there, surrounding Jason.

"Is everything all right?" asked Coach Riley, the leader of the Jupiters. "What's going on?" He wasn't very tall, but he sure had a loud voice!

"No!" yelled Jason. "One of your players stole my lucky mitt!"

There were shouts from the Bandits and the Jupiters. Some of the Bandits began shouting at the Jupiters to give back Jason's glove. The kids started shoving one another. It looked like a fight was about to break out!

"Stop this right now, or I will cancel the game!" said Coach Quinn angrily. "Now, Jason, I'm sure no one stole your mitt. It's probably just lost in the pile of gear here."

"Yeah," said Joe, trying to calm everyone down. "When did you last see your mitt?"

"Right before they got here," said Jason, nodding his head at the Jupiters. "I tossed it on top of my bag, right over there, and then went to practice. The next time I looked over here, he was standing next to my bag!"

Jason pointed to Conor Hound.

"What?" asked Conor. "Are you calling me a thief? I didn't steal your dirty old mitt! I have my own."

"Then why were you standing by my stuff?" asked Jason.

"I was just trying to put my stuff away. I didn't know which pile was ours. But I'm not a thief!"

"Yeah, right! You want to win this game so badly you're willing to cheat!" yelled Jason.

As they spoke, Jason and Conor got closer and closer. Soon they were right next to each other, both angry and shouting. Joe ran in between them.

"Let's look around," said Joe. "Maybe your mitt got lost when other people put their stuff down."

"Right," said Frank. "I'll start looking over here. Jason, why don't you look over there?" Frank pointed as far away from Conor as possible.

"I don't want to hear one word about people stealing," said Coach Quinn. "Is that clear? We'll find your mitt, Jason—but you can't just accuse people of stealing."

Jason nodded. He still looked angry, but he followed Joe over to the other side of the pile of players' bags, bats, balls, and helmets.

Coach Riley called for the Jupiters to go with him.

"Everyone is going to empty out their bags," said the coach. "And if I find Jason's mitt anywhere, that person will be in big trouble. Is that understood?"

The Jupiters nodded and walked away.

"Oh, wow!" said Speedy. "Do you really think Conor took Jason's mitt? What will we do if we can't find it? Jason can't play without it. That would be a disaster!"

Some of the other Bandits were nodding their heads.

"I bet he did take it," said one.

"Yeah!" agreed another. "They'll do anything to win."

"Hey!" said Coach Quinn. "I won't have any more talk like that. You will respect the other team."

"Yes, ma'am," said the Bandits, but it didn't look like everyone agreed with her.

"Good. Because if I catch anyone else accusing someone of stealing without proof, I'll have to ask them not to play."

With that, Coach Quinn walked away. Frank and Joe heard some of their teammates still whispering angrily. But they did it when Coach Quinn wasn't looking.

The Bandits looked through all the gear. They turned bags inside out, looked under baseball caps, and even searched under the bleachers and over by the water cooler. Nothing. This wasn't looking good.

Frank pulled Joe aside.

"Do you think Conor stole Jason's glove?" he asked.

"I don't know," said Joe. "But it doesn't seem to be here."

Jason and some of their other teammates were huddled together, whispering to one another. Occasionally one would angrily point or look in the direction of Conor Hound.

If they didn't find that mitt, Jason wouldn't play. And if he didn't play, the Bandits were definitely going to lose.

Frank and Joe had helped the owner of Fun World find some missing money at a video game contest recently. Maybe they could solve the mystery of what had happened to Jason's mitt—before it was too late!

5

The Six *W*s

While the rest of the Bandits continued to search for Jason's glove, Joe and Frank went over to the bleachers. It was quiet there, so they could think.

"What should we do?" asked Joe.

"You know what Dad says. Start with the six *W*s: What, When, Where, Why, Who, and How."

Joe nodded, remembering that "how" always tripped him up as a *W*. But Frank had explained to him earlier—it did end in a *W*. Frank pulled out a pen and a small spiral-bound notebook from his back pocket. He wrote the words down in big letters on the paper.

WHAT?

Jason's lucky mitt. It was a regular brown baseball glove, a little larger than most. It was old and beat-up looking.

"Do you think someone could have taken it by accident?" asked Joe. "Like, maybe they thought it was theirs?"

Frank thought for a second. "No," he said. "It's bigger than any of our mitts. And remember, it had 'Winner' stitched on it? As soon as someone saw that, they'd know."

Joe took the notebook and drew the mitt, complete with the word "Winner" on it. Now they would have something to show witnesses!

WHEN?

"Hey, Jason!" called Joe. Jason had stopped picking through the pile of bats and balls. He was sitting by himself on the other side of the bleachers. He still looked angry. When Joe called his name, he came running over.

"Are you guys going to find my mitt?" asked Jason excitedly.

"We're trying," said Joe. "But we need your help. Do you remember when you last had it?"

"Well," said Jason, "I don't know exactly. I got here around eight thirty, and I guess I put my bag down right away. But I knew everyone would want to touch the lucky mitt, so I kept that with me. Then, when it was time to practice, I threw it in with the rest of my stuff—right before you guys arrived. When was that?"

Frank looked at his watch. "Eight fifty-nine exactly," he said. Then he wrote, *8:59—Jason threw the mitt onto the pile.*

"Okay," said Joe. "And when did you find out the mitt was missing?"

"Right after Coach Quinn called a break."

Mitt discovered missing at about 10:00, Frank wrote in the book.

"Did anything strange happen in between those times?" asked Frank.

"No," said Jason. "We were practicing, and then the Jupiters showed up. I saw Conor standing around our stuff, and after that my mitt was gone! I'm sure he stole it."

Jupiters arrived at 9:30, wrote Frank.

"I think Conor stole my mitt because he knows I'm better than he is!" said Jason, getting angry again. "Are you guys going to catch him?"

"We don't know he stole it," said Frank. "But we're going to catch whoever did!"

Frank didn't want to assume that Conor had taken Jason's mitt. But it wasn't looking good for the Jupiters' first baseman.

WHERE?

"We need to look at the crime scene again," said Joe. "Now that everybody's back to practicing, maybe we can find some clues." The game was still on, so the Jupiters and the Bandits were all getting ready, except for Jason.

Frank and Joe walked back over to the place where Jason had last seen his mitt. But so many people had touched things, it was impossible to tell if anything was out of order.

There were a million footprints everywhere. But no suspicious trails or anything. Frank and Joe walked around the pile, each in a different direction, to make sure they didn't miss anything.

"Did you find anything?" asked Joe when they had walked all the way around to the other side.

"Just this," said Frank, holding out a large stick. "It was mixed up with all the gear."

"It is random," said Joe. "But do you think it has anything to do with Jason's mitt?"

"I don't know," said Frank. "But I'm writing it down anyway, just in case."

Found at scene: gear, footprints, one large stick, wrote Frank in his notebook.

"We're not getting anywhere!" said Joe.

He was right. They had nothing.

WHY?

"We know that the person who took Jason's mitt did it on purpose," said Frank, "because they couldn't have mistaken the lucky mitt for theirs."

 42

"Right," said Joe. "Maybe the Jupiters *would* do anything to win. . . ."

"Is there any reason anyone else would have taken it?" asked Frank.

"Everyone on the team loves Jason," said Joe. "And we all want to win this game. I can't think of any reason someone else would have stolen the mitt. Can you?"

Frank shook his head. Nothing else made sense.

"Wait!" said Frank. "What if someone wanted to sell it? I bet they could get a lot of money for a mitt that used to belong to Willy 'Winner' Prime."

"That's true. So it's either Conor Hound . . . or anyone! We're not getting any closer."

WHO?

That was the big question. The more evidence they found, the more it seemed that Conor—or one of the other Jupiters—was guilty. Conor had the opportunity, and a reason for doing it. But they couldn't be sure.

They needed a witness, or solid proof. That was what their dad had taught them.

"You need proof, not just a good suspicion," he'd said. Joe and Frank just hoped they could find some proof before the game began at nine thirty. Time was running out.

HOW?

Good question! But they wouldn't know the answer to this one until they found out who had taken the mitt.

Suddenly a voice broke in on them.

"Hey, Frank! Hey, Joe! Shouldn't you be practicing?"

Before they could look to see who it was, some-one tackled Frank from behind.

WHOOMPH!

Frank was knocked to the ground in a heap!

6

A Surprise Witness!

"Oh no! I'm sorry, boys." Mr. Mack had walked over as quickly as he could. Lucy had Frank pinned to the ground. She licked his face all over. Frank tried to tell Lucy to get off, but the dog was tickling him so much he couldn't get a word out. Joe was laughing so hard he had to sit down.

"Lucy! Down, girl. Down!"

Finally Mr. Mack was able to pull his dog off Frank.

"Gosh, Frank, I'm sorry," said Mr. Mack. "Every time we see you, we knock you down! I hope you're not hurt."

"It's okay, Mr. Mack. I'm fine," said Frank.

"That was the funniest thing I've seen all day," said Joe. He laughed as Frank finally got up off the ground and brushed the dirt off his uniform.

To show there were no hard feelings, Frank called Lucy over and patted her on the head.

"Watch out, Frank—it's that stick you've got. Lucy thinks that means you're going to play fetch. That's why she tackled you. I was wondering where she'd dropped that stick—we were playing with it earlier."

Lucy leaped up on Frank again. She was so big, her paws were on Frank's shoulders.

"Here you go, girl!" Frank gave Lucy the stick. She raced off into the woods behind the baseball diamond, back near where they had first seen her and Mr. Mack earlier that morning.

"Where's she going?" Joe asked Mr. Mack.

"Oh, Lucy buries her sticks off in the woods. Then she goes back and digs them up. Then she buries them again. It's a game she likes to play. She'll be back in a few minutes."

"So, what are you guys doing out here still?" asked Joe. He'd picked up the notebook Frank had dropped when Lucy tackled him. Over his shoulder, Frank could see his brother writing the words *Possible suspect: Mr. Mack.*

"I watch all the Bayport Bandits' games! I'm a huge baseball fan," said Mr. Mack. "I can't get too close to the field, though, because Lucy would chase the balls out on the field!"

"Are you a big fan of Winner Prime?" asked Joe. Frank could see him writing the word "motive" in the notebook. Maybe Mr. Mack was such a big baseball fan that he wanted the mitt for himself!

"Who, Jason's father? I'd heard he played baseball, but I don't follow the major leagues, just the

49

local teams. I used to be a Little League coach myself, about forty years ago."

Joe crossed out the word "motive." It didn't seem like Mr. Mack was their suspect. He was just a fan. Besides, if he had the mitt, the boys would see it. He didn't even have a bag with him. With his cane, he couldn't have run away and hidden the mitt.

All around them, the families of the players on both teams were beginning to arrive. Some sat on the bleachers, and others brought blankets and had picnics out by the field. Joe and Frank waved to their parents, who had taken up their usual spot on a blanket near the Bandits' bench so they could watch both Joe and Frank at the same time.

Pretty soon the game was going to start, and they were no closer to finding Jason's mitt. The boys wanted to go ask their dad what he thought, but this was their case. They preferred to figure it out on their own. They'd done so well with the missing money at the video game contest, after all.

Meanwhile, Mr. Mack kept talking. He loved baseball so much, it seemed like he could go on all day. "Yup, Lucy and I are here every game. We usually watch from back behind the bleachers. I tie her up to one of the posts."

Mr. Mack pointed back behind where Jason had been sitting. From there, he would have had a great view of the Bandits' gear.

"Hey," said Frank. "Were you around earlier?"

"We've been here since right after we ran into you."

"Did you see anyone over by our stuff?"

Mr. Mack shook his head. "Just the team. Lucy ran onto the field and then kept going—I had to chase after her."

That would explain the stick they'd found, thought Frank. So now they had no clues at all.

"You didn't see anyone else?" asked Joe.

"Nope. Oh, wait! I did—that big kid, over there. He was looking through the stuff a little while ago."

Mr. Mack pointed across the field—directly at Conor Hound!

"Well, the game is going to start soon," said Mr. Mack. "I should go find Lucy and get ready to watch. Good luck, boys!" He patted Joe and Frank on the shoulder and headed off toward the woods.

The brothers looked at each other. All the evidence pointed in the same direction—Conor Hound! They needed to go to the source. And that meant talking to Conor.

They started to head across the field. But then a whistle blew.

"Line up!" shouted Coach Quinn.

The game was about to begin!

7

Strike Three, You're Out!

Oh no! The game was beginning, and they still hadn't figured out who had taken Jason's mitt—they hadn't even talked to their best suspect. They would just have to find a way to get to Conor during the game.

Frank and Joe rushed to get ready. They grabbed their mitts and headed over to the Bandits' dugout. All the players on both teams were doing the same—all except Jason, who refused to play.

"Not without my lucky mitt!" he said. "This

game is unfair! They're winning by cheating." But Coach Quinn wouldn't listen to him.

"No one is cheating," she said. "Your mitt was lost. It's terrible, but it wasn't anyone's fault. A good sportsman would play no matter what."

But Jason was too mad to listen to her. Instead, he sat on the bench with his hands folded across his chest, looking angry.

Coach Quinn tried to convince him to play. She asked Jason if his father would act that way in a game. She told him that the team was depending on him. But there was no getting through to Jason. Finally the coach shrugged her shoulders. She hoped he would decide to play, but the game would go on—with or without him.

The whole team tried to get Jason to play, but it was no use. Jason refused. And without their best player, the Bandits didn't stand a chance. Frank and Joe had seven innings—like most Little League teams, the Bandits' games lasted seven innings rather than nine like the pros—to find the missing mitt . . . or else!

Once the players were ready, the two coaches met in the center of the field. They shook hands and flipped a coin to see which team would be up at bat first.

"Call it," said Coach Quinn.

"Tails!" said Coach Riley.

It was tails. The Jupiters would bat first. The Bandits took their places around the field. Frank stayed by home plate. He put on the chest guard that protected him against any balls that got past the batter. It was a big piece of plastic, and it was heavy and clunky. But Frank was happy to wear it. Without that and his face mask, he'd have no protection from Speedy's wicked fastballs!

Since Jason wouldn't play, Joe had been moved to first base. To cover second base, they'd moved Ellie Freeman from the outfield. She was a good player, but she'd never played second base before. It was going to be a tough game.

"Strike three, you're out!"

The umpire pointed the second Jupiter player back to the bench. So far, thanks to Speedy, the

Bandits were doing okay. The first batter had popped the ball straight up into the air, and Frank had caught it, putting him out. Speedy had just struck out the second batter. One more and it would be the Bandits' turn at bat. Maybe they could make it without Jason after all.

The third batter stepped up to the plate. He was big. Not as big as Conor, but big.

The first pitch was a foul ball, off to the side. But the second was right down the middle, and the batter hit it with all his strength.

CRAAACK!!

The ball flew toward center field. The batter had aimed right for the hole in the outfield where Ellie used to stand. The other outfielders scrambled to try to catch it, but they were spread too thin. If someone had been there, it would have been an easy out. Instead, the batter made it all the way to third base!

Things had just gone from okay to bad for the Bandits. And they were about to get worse!

The next batter hit a low line drive up the middle, right past Speedy. The shortstop snapped it up on the first hop. The first runner was already nearing home. They weren't going to get him out.

"Throw it to first!" Ellie yelled to the shortstop.

But the player hesitated a moment too long before throwing the ball to Joe, and the Jupiter batter made it to the base safely.

By the end of the second inning, the score was Jupiters 4, Bandits 2. The Bandits needed to get Jason back on the team—and that meant finding his mitt.

Finally, as the third inning was about to start, Frank got a chance to talk to Conor, who was first up at bat.

"Hey," said Frank.

Conor just stared at him.

"You're Conor Hound, right?"

"Yeah," said Conor.

"I'm Frank Hardy." Frank pulled up his face mask. "I heard you have the most RBIs in the entire league!" Their dad had taught them that people are more likely to answer questions when you put them in a good mood.

Conor smiled. "Yep!" he said.

"That's awesome. Can I ask you a question?"

"Sure," said Conor.

"Why were you over by the pile of gear earlier?"

"WHAT?" said Conor. "I told everybody, I didn't steal that mitt!"

"I wasn't saying—"

But Conor cut him off. "I'm not a thief! And I don't need to cheat to win some dumb game."

"Boys!" called Coach Quinn. "What is going on over here?"

"He accused me of stealing!" said Conor, pointing at Frank.

"Frank, is this true?"

"No! I was just asking why he was over by our gear."

Frank could tell by the look on her face that Coach Quinn didn't believe him.

"Frank, I'm disappointed. This is very unlike you. I'm going to have to ask you to sit out the rest of this game. Please take off the catcher's gear so we can find someone to replace you."

Frank could barely believe what he had heard. He wasn't accusing Conor of cheating—he was just trying to find out what had happened. But Coach Quinn wouldn't listen.

"But, Coach Quinn, we were just trying to

help!" cried Joe. The entire team had gathered around to see what was happening.

"You were involved with this too, Joe?" asked Coach Quinn.

"Yes, ma'am," he said.

"Then I'm afraid you're going to sit out the game as well."

Things were going from bad to worse!

8

Triple Play

Sidelined? In the biggest game of the year? How could this be happening? Frank couldn't believe how bad their luck had been. He watched as another Bandit put on the catcher's gear and the team got ready to start again. Conor Hound gave him an angry look.

Joe tried to argue with Coach Quinn, but it was no use. Their parents came over to see what all the fuss was about.

"What happened, Joe?" asked Mr. Hardy.

"It wasn't our fault!" said Joe. "Frank was just trying to ask Conor about Jason's mitt, and—"

"Yeah!" chimed in Frank. "And Joe was just trying to get Coach Quinn to understand, but—"

"Slow down, boys," said Mrs. Hardy.

"Yes," said Mr. Hardy. "Now, start at the beginning."

While the Bayport Bandits tried to figure out who would fill the two new holes on the field, Frank and Joe told their parents what had happened. When they were done, Mr. Hardy shook his head.

"Do you think Conor stole Jason's mitt?" asked Mr. Hardy.

Frank and Joe hesitated.

"No," said Frank. "I think he's innocent. He seems pretty upset about it. And from everything I've heard about him, he's a good ballplayer. He wouldn't need to cheat to do well."

"Well," said Mr. Hardy. "It seems like the only

thing to do is figure out where Jason's mitt really is. If you can do that before the game ends, maybe Coach Quinn will understand that you were just trying to help."

"But we don't even have a suspect," said Frank.

"You know what that means. You have to go back over your evidence. Talk to your witnesses. Facts are what solve crimes, boys."

Frank and Joe nodded. Mr. and Mrs. Hardy went back to their blanket to watch the rest of the game. The boys pulled out their notebook.

"The only people who knew anything were Jason and Mr. Mack," said Frank. "So maybe we should talk to them again."

"Good idea," said Joe. "Let's talk to Mr. Mack first."

Together, they walked back behind the bleachers, to the corner where Mr. Mack and Lucy were sitting. Lucy was tied to a post to keep her from chasing the balls, but she wagged her tail when the boys came over.

"Shouldn't you boys be playing?" asked Mr. Mack.

Frank and Joe explained what had happened.

"That's terrible!" Mr. Mack said. "But I don't know if I can help you. I really didn't see anyone go over by the gear except for that boy from the other team, Jason, and myself. Like I said, Lucy ran away after that, so I had to go look for her."

The boys thanked Mr. Mack for his help and set off to find Jason. He was their last hope.

"We must be missing something," said Joe.

"I know," said Frank. "But what?"

The fourth inning was just beginning as they neared the baseball field again. The Bandits were now behind 5–2. Frank and Joe watched for a few minutes. Missing three players made it almost impossible for the team to play. The Johnston Jupiters practically owned the field. This was going to be one of the worst defeats in Little League history!

The boys went to find Jason. They couldn't stand to watch the team lose so badly.

"That is totally unfair!" Jason said before Frank or Joe could even say hi. "And it's all Conor's fault! First he steals my mitt, and now he's got Coach Quinn on his side."

"We don't think Conor stole your mitt," Frank told him.

"You don't?" replied Jason. "Then if he didn't, who did?"

"That's what we're trying to figure out. Do you remember anything else—anything that might help us figure out where your mitt went?"

"No! I already told you everything."

"Think hard," said Joe. "Finding that mitt is the only way to get us all back on the team—and the Bandits need us!"

Jason looked over at the field just as the Bandits' new first baseman dropped the ball, let-

ting Conor Hound run safely to second. Jason scrunched up his face and tried to remember everything he could.

"Like I told you, nothing really happened. I got here, I dropped off my stuff, that stupid dog jumped on me, I threw my lucky mitt on top of my bag, and then I went to practice. That's it."

"Wait a second," said Frank. He was remembering something. "Lucy jumped on you?"

"Yeah," said Jason.

"Was this before or after you threw your mitt down?"

"Before, I think."

Frank looked excited.

"Joe, don't you remember what Mr. Mack said? He said that Lucy jumped on me because she wanted the stick I was holding. She thought we were going to play fetch. If Jason threw down his mitt right after Lucy jumped on him . . ."

"Lucy must have thought Jason wanted to play. That's why she left her stick behind!"

"Lucy took the mitt!" both boys yelled at the same time.

"Strike three!" announced the umpire. The top of the fourth was over. The boys had only a few more innings to get the mitt and save the game!

9

Deep in the Outfield

Jason," yelled Frank and Joe. "We know where your mitt is!"

"You do? Where?"

"Follow us!"

The boys took off. They had to see Mr. Mack and get the mitt back from Lucy.

"Hi again!" said Mr. Mack as the boys ran up to him. "My, you boys sure are running around a lot."

"Mr. Mack," said Joe. "Lucy took Jason's mitt!"

"What?" asked Mr. Mack.

"Lucy must have thought Jason wanted to play fetch when he threw it down with the rest of the gear. She took it!"

"Oh no," said Mr. Mack, looking very concerned. "I'm so sorry! I'm sure she didn't hurt it. She's very careful with her toys."

"Bad girl," he said to Lucy. Lucy whimpered guiltily.

"That's all right," said Jason. "I just want to get it back so we can play in the game! Where do you think she put it?"

"Oh, dear," said Mr. Mack. "I don't know. She runs too fast for me to keep up with her. She buries sticks and toys out in the woods behind the baseball field, but I don't know where. Only Lucy knows that."

Jason, the Hardys, and Mr. Mack all turned to look at Lucy. Lucy whined and put her head between her paws. Frank and Joe had finally found the culprit—but they'd never be able to get her to talk!

"What are we going to do now?" asked Jason. "Maybe if you explain everything, Coach Quinn will let you guys play, but I still won't have my mitt. I can't play without it."

"We're not giving up yet," said Joe. "I have an idea."

Joe ran back toward the Bandits' dugout.

"Where's he going?" asked Mr. Mack.

"I don't know," said Frank.

Joe returned with his own mitt in hand.

"Mr. Mack, can you untie Lucy?"

Mr. Mack set Lucy free. Joe held the mitt high in the air, above Lucy's head. She jumped up on Joe, trying to get at the mitt.

"Here, girl," Joe said. "Go get it!"

He threw the mitt as hard as he could. Lucy ran

a few feet. She jumped in the air and grabbed the
mitt with her teeth. Then she took off running,
past the outfield, toward the deep woods.

"Follow that dog!" Joe shouted.

"Be careful, boys! Good luck!" called Mr. Mack, as Joe, Frank, and Jason all chased after Lucy.

Lucy was fast! First she ran straight toward the crowd of people watching the game on their picnic blankets. She leaped right over two little kids and nearly knocked over a giant bottle of soda. The boys had no choice but to run right after her, apologizing the whole way.

"Excuse me! Sorry!" said Frank.

"Coming through!" said Joe.

Jason took one look at the mess made by Lucy, Frank, and Joe and decided to jump over the entire picnic blanket. He took one big leap and landed safely on the other side.

Lucy's tail was wagging now. She was enjoying the chase. She stopped for a second, then turned around and looked at the boys. She crouched down on her front legs, the mitt still in her mouth. It looked like she was smiling at them. She waited until the boys got just close enough to grab her. Joe reached out—and Lucy hopped out of his way.

Joe stumbled and fell.

"You all right?" asked Frank.

Joe nodded. Lucy was sitting there, just a few feet away. Frank and Jason both jumped at her at the same time. But again, Lucy dodged out of the way.

THUD!

Frank and Jason slammed right into each other. They landed in a big heap on the ground. Joe had to help them both up. Lucy barked once, almost dropping the mitt, and then bounded away.

She ran straight for the trees. The boys tried

to keep up, but their two legs were no match for Lucy's four.

"We have to keep up!" shouted Jason. He put on a burst of speed and managed to pass Frank and Joe.

When she got to the edge of the woods, Lucy paused. It was almost as though she was waiting for the boys to reach her. Jason made it first, with Frank and Joe close behind. Lucy slipped in among the trees.

Now running was harder. There were roots and rocks everywhere. The boys had to dodge around trees and bushes. Lucy disappeared and reappeared. The boys kept as close to her as they could. But finally Lucy disappeared for good.

"Where did she go?" asked Joe.

The boys all stood still and looked around. They couldn't see the dog anywhere.

"Oh no!" said Jason.

"Shhh . . ." Frank held his finger up to his lips. The boys got quiet. In the distance they could hear the sound of digging.

"This way!" Frank took off running deeper into the woods. He could hear Lucy in front of him, though he couldn't see her yet. Suddenly the ground disappeared beneath him!

"Whoa!" he shouted. He had reached the edge of a drop in the woods. There was a five-foot-deep hole in front of him. He threw his arms out to try to keep his balance. But it was no use. He started to fall!

"Careful!"

Jason grabbed the back of Frank's shirt and pulled him away from the edge of the hole.

"Thanks," said Frank.

"Look!" Joe pointed down into the hole. At

the bottom was Lucy, digging the hole deeper. All around her was stuff—balls and sticks and toys and Frisbees . . . and Jason's mitt!

"We found it!" Jason shouted.

10

Secret File #2: A Home Run!

Lucy wasn't happy when the boys took both of the mitts back, but she didn't try to stop them either.

"Time to go back to Mr. Mack, girl?" said Joe.

Lucy barked twice. Then she picked up a stick and ran back toward the field.

"Good girl!" called Jason. Now that he had his lucky mitt back, he was happy again—and ready to go play!

"Do you think the game is still going on?"

asked Jason. "Will we make it back in time?"

"Hmmm," said Frank. "The average batter takes two minutes. There are usually five batters on each side for every inning. I would say there should be two innings left!"

"Awesome!" yelled Joe. "Let's go."

The boys ran out of the woods as fast as they could. This time, they ran straight through the bushes. All they cared about was getting back as soon as possible. When they got out, Mr. Mack was waiting for them, with Lucy beside him.

"Did you find your mitt?" he asked.

"Yes!" all three boys shouted at the same time. They kept running.

When they made it back to the baseball diamond, the Jupiters were leaving the field.

"Uh-oh," said Jason. "Are we too late?"

The boys ran over to Coach Quinn.

"Is the game over?" asked Jason.

"No, but I'm afraid it's not going so well. We're down four runs, and there are only two innings left. Where did you boys go?"

"Frank and Joe found my mitt!" said Jason. "Lucy stole it!"

"That's great news!" said Coach Quinn. "But who's Lucy?" She looked out at the players of the two teams.

"*That's* Lucy," said Joe, pointing over to the bleachers where Mr. Mack and Lucy were sitting.

"She thought Jason was playing fetch," Frank explained. "So she grabbed the mitt and buried it in the woods with her other toys."

"So you boys really were just trying to find Jason's mitt. I guess I owe you an apology. How about I give it to you . . . *after* you get ready to play? It's the top of the sixth, and the team needs you!"

The three boys cheered.

"Wait," said Jason. "There's something I have to do first."

Jason walked over to where the Jupiters were sitting. He went right up to Conor Hound. They talked for a few minutes. Then they shook hands.

Jason came back over to Joe, Frank, and Coach Quinn.

"I had to apologize for accusing him of stealing," Jason said.

"That's very grown-up of you, Jason," said the coach. "I'm proud to have you on the Bandits." She shook his hand too.

Then a big smile lit up Jason's face. "And I also said I'm sorry that we're totally going to beat them!"

Even Coach Quinn had to laugh at that.

When the rest of the Bandits saw Joe, Frank, and Jason getting ready to play, they gave a huge cheer—and so did the crowd! The Bandits fans had given up on their team winning, but now they were excited again.

"Coach Quinn is letting you guys play? That's awesome! We're totally going to win now. I can't wait to write this all up in my blog tonight. This has been the most exciting game ever." Speedy was talking so fast it was almost impossible to understand a word she was saying. The boys would have to check out her blog tomorrow to find out.

The sixth inning was about to start. Frank took back the catcher's gear and got suited up. Jason took his regular place on first base, and Joe went back to second. Now there were no more holes in the outfield for the Jupiters to aim for.

The first three Jupiters up at bat were knocked out one after another. Speedy struck out one,

Jason tagged another, and Frank caught a foul ball hit by the third. Now it was the Bandits' turn at bat. With a little luck, they could narrow the score.

In the bottom of the inning, Jason, Frank, and Joe were the first three batters up.

Bam!

Bam!

Bam!

Jason slammed a double, and Frank followed with a home run. Just like that, the Bandits had scored two runs. On his turn, Joe hit a line drive into the outfield. Now he was on third base, waiting for the chance to score another. It was 8–6. The Bandits were still behind, but they were catching up!

Speedy batted next. The Jupiters were expecting a big hit to try to score another run, but

Speedy tricked them—she bunted! Before they could figure out what to do, Jason was safe at home, and Speedy was on first base. 8–7!

Speedy stole second base while the Jupiters struck out the next Bandit batter. A lucky catch knocked out another Bandit, but Speedy managed to get to third base.

"Go Speedy! Go Speedy! Go Speedy!" the crowd chanted.

She smiled and waved, just waiting for her chance to score another run for the Bandits. The next batter got a hit and tried to make it to second, but was tagged out—but not before Speedy crossed home plate! Now the score was tied, 8–8, and there was only one inning to go.

"Do you think we can do it?" Coach Quinn asked the team.

"Yeah!" the Bandits shouted. They were in this to win.

The Jupiters batted at the top of the seventh. Speedy struck out the first two batters, but then it was Conor's turn at bat. He took a few practice swings. He looked bigger than ever. Frank crouched down in his catcher's gear and hoped that Speedy could strike him out too. But no such luck. He hit a hard ground ball on his first swing.

The ball was headed right between first and second base. Joe and Jason both ran to get it.

"Go, Joe!" screamed Frank.

Joe leaned down to get the ball—but Jason got there first. He scooped the ball up with one swipe of his lucky mitt and ran back to first base, but it was too late. Conor was safe.

It took two more batters, but eventually the Jupiters brought Conor home. Now they were ahead, 9–8. The Bandits had only one chance left to win the game.

But the Jupiters were not going to go down easy. They struck out the Bandits' first two batters in the bottom of the seventh. Now everything depended on their next batter—Jason!

The crowd chanted his name. Frank and Joe sat on the edge of the bench, leaning forward for a better view.

Jason bent his knees and pulled the bat back behind his shoulder in a perfect batting stance. The first pitch came. Jason swung—and missed!

"Strike one!" the umpire called.

The Bandits fans shouted, "Go, Jason!" Jason got back into position. The second pitch came. Again he swung.

And again he missed.

This time the crowd was silent. If he missed again, it was all over. The Bandits would lose this year's Little League championship.

Time seemed to slow down as the Jupiters' pitcher got ready. He wound up. He threw. The ball seemed to hang in the air. Jason pulled the bat back.

CRAAACK!!

Just like that, the ball was flying up over the heads of the Jupiters, past the outfield, over the parents on their picnic blankets. Up, up, and away!

Joe, Frank, and the rest of the Bandits leaped to their feet, cheering and screaming.

It was a home run! The score was tied at 9–9.

And tied it remained. No matter how hard they tried, neither team could score another run. The game went into extra innings, and then extra-extra innings. Finally the coaches called a time-out.

"Maybe it's time to call it a tie?" Coach Quinn said.

The Bandits thought about it. It would mean sharing the trophy, but the Jupiters were good players—maybe just as good as they were. Maybe both teams deserved to win.

"What do you guys think?" asked Coach Quinn. "Should we declare it a tie?"

"Yeah," said Joe and Frank at the same time. That seemed fair to them. The rest of the Bandits nodded in agreement.

"You guys are the best team a coach could have," she said.

When the two coaches announced the tie, everyone in the audience cheered. This was the best Little League championship game ever!

When Joe and Frank returned home, they were exhausted—but they still had one thing left to finish.

The boys waited until their parents were safely inside and then made a dash for their tree house. They passed the side of the house, and the garage, above which Mr. Hardy had been fixing up a spare room.

"Watch out!" Frank called.

There was a ladder leaning up against the garage, and Frank's warning came just in time to save Joe from tripping over it.

"Jump!" warned Joe, and Frank just missed tripping over a couple of paint cans that were lying outside, probably for the spare room.

When the boys reached the woods on the edge of their backyard, they looked around furtively and ducked in. Finally they'd reached their destination.

Frank pulled the ladder down from the tree house with the pulley so they could climb in. Once they were both inside, Frank handed Joe a big green marker.

"I got to do it last time," Frank said. "It's your turn."

Joe's face exploded into a grin, and he walked over to the big white dry-erase board hanging on the tree house wall. Then he began writing:

SECRET FILES
THE HARDY BOYS®

Follow the trail with Frank and Joe Hardy
in this new chapter book mystery series!

BY FRANKLIN W. DIXON

FROM ALADDIN • PUBLISHED BY
SIMON & SCHUSTER

MORE TOTALLY TERRIFYING TALES FROM AWARD-WINNING AUTHOR
JAMES HOWE

From Aladdin
Published by Simon & Schuster

Nancy Drew and The Clue Crew

Test your detective skills with more Clue Crew cases!

FROM ALADDIN • PUBLISHED BY SIMON & SCHUSTER

MORE ANIMAL BOOKS FROM AWARD-WINNING AUTHOR

Bill Wallace

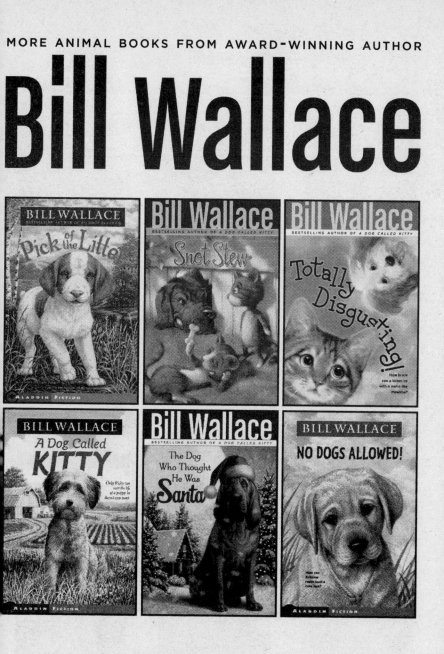